Gay Interracial Romance

LOVELY BOY

DEXTER CHASE

WARNING

This book contains sexually explicit scenes and adult language. It may be considered offensive to some readers. This book is for sale to adults ONLY.

Please store your files wisely where they cannot be accessed by underage readers.

* * * * * * * * * * * * * * * * * * *

WANT FREE COPIES OF MY BOOKS?
Just visit my blog and download free copies of my books:
http://dexter-chase.awesomeauthors.org/dexter-chase/

About the Publisher

4Fun Publishing, a member of BLVNP Incorporated, 340 S. Lemon #6200, Walnut CA 91789, info@blvnp.com / legal@blvnp.com

NOTE: Due to the highly emotional reaction of some people to works of erotic fiction, any email sent to the above address that contains foul language or religious references is automatically deleted by our anti-spam software and will not be seen. All other communications are welcome.

DISCLAIMER

Please don't be stupid and kill yourself. This book is a work of FICTION. Do not try any new sexual practice that you find in this book. It is fiction and not to be confused with reality. Neither the author nor the publisher or its associates assume any responsibility for any loss, injury, death or legal consequences resulting from acting on the contents in this book. Every character in this book is over 18 years of age. The author's opinions are not to be construed as the opinions of the publisher. The material in this book is for entertainment purposes ONLY. Enjoy.

Lovely Boy
Gay Interracial Romance

By: Dexter Chase

© Dexter Chase 2015
ISBN: 978-1-68030-462-6

Chapter 1

Ciriaco walked into his first period lesson, alone and friendless as he had been for the last year. He didn't know why his classmates continued to ignore him. He had been branded Japanese on his first day and that was enough to isolate him. He had tried to tell them that Ciriaco S. Calalang was hardly a Japanese name, and that the language he spoke was Tagalog because he was from the Philippines.

It didn't do any good—they had made up their minds and that was it. He had even assumed the English name of Sam to try to fit in, but it didn't change anything.

But by any yardstick, this Filipino boy was stunning. Tall for his age and race at this period in time, he was five feet eleven inches tall with a well-defined and attractive body. Between his legs nestled a penis that would never disgrace him for its size, and he was a fine athlete. Academically, he surprised his teachers. They had expected him to be worse than his peers because he had come from a war torn region where continued education would have been patchy.

The reason for the animosity was that this was the year 1946, and the war in the Pacific had only been over for a few months. Ciriaco was one of the few refugees that the British government had taken from the Philippines after their liberation, and he had been placed in this all-boys school as a boarder. Everyone knew of the brutality of the Japanese towards POWs and many of them had died in captivity. The sons of some of those men were also at this school.

The only positive thing was that he was never bullied, possibly because he was big enough to defend himself. He shared a dormitory with fifteen other boys, but they had pushed his bed and locker well away from everyone else. This was like a punch in the stomach for him. He was a sensitive and friendly guy who had tried so hard to be friends with his class and dorm mates, but all he had met with was rejection. He had turned out for sports, being selected for the school team and athletic squad. He was a star student, always ready to help a class mate, but always having his offers of help rejected. Into his final year before university, he had spent a miserable Christmas with one of the masters and came back thinking about his last two terms and what would happen to him after that. A new boy appeared in his dormitory and in his classes on the first day of the new term.

Sam was in love the second he set eyes on this new addition. He watched as he entered and presented a note to his teacher. The teacher spoke a few words to him quietly and then looked up and surveyed his class.

"Not much choice Affleck, you will have to sit next to Calalang," pointing at the desk next to Sam, that as always was unoccupied.

Sam nodded to him as he sat down and then tried to concentrate on the lesson. Difficult, because this vision was so close. Lesson ended and as they were packing up their books, Phill put out his hand, and with a warm smile on his face, faced Sam.

"I'm Phill Affleck, pleased to meet you."

Sam blushed. This hadn't happened to him since he came here.

"I'm Ciriaco Calalang, but you can call me Sam."

"Oh, hi Sam, you're Filipino aren't you?"

Sam grinned. "Yes, but how did you know?"

"My dad was based in your country after it was liberated. He flew most of his combat missions from there. He was a bomber pilot."

"You're American, aren't you?"

"Yeah, my old man has been drafted here as a liaison officer with the Royal Air Force. He spends a lot of time away, so he thought it would be better for me to go to a boarding school. I don't mind. I did the same in the States after my mom died. What about you?"

"Not much to tell, really. My whole family was wiped out in a Japanese attack and I was brought to England. I have no relatives so they stuck me here. I stay with a teacher every holiday."

Phill grinned then and said, "We'll have to see if we can change that next vacation. I guess we had better head out for our next lesson."

They walked together to their next class and Sam kept taking sidelong glances at his new and only friend. He knew that there was a chance he would keep him because he knew he was not Japanese. He also knew that it would be purgatory being close to Phill. To Sam, this American boy was sex on legs. He had a little boy face but it was absolutely enchanting to look at. There was nothing "little boy" about anything else to do with him.

They had P.E. that day and Sam saw his new friend naked as they changed for sport. *Stunning* didn't even come close to defining this boy in Sam's eyes. His eyes watered as he looked, he could hardly take his eyes off him.

Sam had to dress very quickly after the view he had seen. His cock went into overdrive hard, fortunately only Phill saw it. He gasped— Sam's hard cock was a sight to behold, even if he had only caught a glimpse of it.

When they returned to their dormitory, Sam was surprised to see his bed and locker close up to the next one and an additional one the other side that he found out was Phill's. At the other end of the dorm, most of the other boys were in a huddle, occasionally looking back at Sam and Phill. Eventually they moved down the room, and with heads down, listened as their designated leader looked at Sam and put out his hand.

"Sam, we all want to apologise for the way we have treated you this last year. We really did believe that you were Japanese, and several of us lost our fathers in prison camps, so you were the enemy. Phill has shown us the error of our ways. Please forgive us and be our friend."

Sam was delighted. All of the misery of the last year fell away and he shook hands willingly. For the next several minutes his back was pounded and his hand was nearly wrung off. The happy tears were a measure of Sam's feelings. In one day, he had met a boy he loved instantly and a dorm full of new friends—at last.

There were no assignments this first day of term, so after supper both boys showered and then sat around the recreation room chatting. Sam was amazed that Phill didn't put any clothes on. He sat in an armchair opposite Sam, with his feet up displaying his wares. Of course Sam was instantly as hard as an iron bar. Despite the fact that he was clothed, his erection showed and Phill grinned.

"I can put some clothes on if my nakedness worries you."

He was looking at Sam's bulging trousers as he said it. Sam blushed almost scarlet and stuttered a reply.

"No you're fine. Are you used to sitting around naked?"

"Yes, I never used to dress after supper in my old school because we had to do our own laundry, so I just made sure I didn't have very much."

During the next few weeks, Sam couldn't remember a time in his life when he spent so much time with an erection. Phill was a constant source of agony to him. The boy appeared to be totally uninhibited and comfortable in his skin. Undressing for a shower one evening, when the dormitory was empty, Phill noticed Sam's usual erection and decided to be cheeky. He stripped completely, showing Sam his butt and then turned round displaying an erection as well. It was long and slim with a well-proportioned ball sac below.

That was too much for Sam. He burst into tears, shocking Phill who moved in quickly and grabbed Sam in a hug.

"I'm sorry Sam, what is it? What did I do?"

All reserve gone, Sam was so devastated he just blurted out his feelings.

"I love you so much, I have dreamt about seeing you like this since the first day. I think you are so beautiful."

Phill was shaken. He pulled away and saw the devastated look in Sam's eyes. Before Sam could react, Phill grabbed him again and whispered in his ear.

"Don't cry Sam, I think I love you too."

With tears still streaming down his face, Sam pulled away again to look at him.

"Do you mean that?"

Phill nodded.

Sam sank onto his bed.

"I never thought in a million years you would feel the same as me. I really do think you are beautiful. It was very easy for me to fall in love with you because you are such a beautiful person inside as well."

Phill laughed—he couldn't have been happier, here was a boy that he could love. Of course he loved his dad, but they saw so little of each other and he did love a cuddle. Now it looked as though he could get one.

Agony was the word that described these two boys' state of mind for the next few weeks because they could find no place to express their love in a physical way. Phill however was working on the half term break. His father was going to be home, so he asked if he would sign as guardian for a friend so that he could spend the holiday.

The telephone conversation between father and son was interesting.

"Hi Dad."

"Hi Phill, how are you?"

"I'm fine, school is good and I've made a special friend. That's who I want to talk about. He is a Filipino and he's an orphan. He has nowhere to stay when we go on half term break. Can he stay with us?"

"That will be a little difficult. You know the Brits have only given me a two bedroom house. They are pretty short of housing since their war finished."

"That's okay, he can sleep with me."

"Why would you want a friend to sleep with you?"

"Because he's my best friend and he has nowhere else to go."

"I'll have to think about this son. I might need to go away while you are home, and I would take you with me if it was just you."

"Please Dad, I won't mind staying at home. Sam and I can look after ourselves."

Major Affleck could hear the desperation in his son's voice.

"He's really special, is he?"

"Yes Dad, the most special friend I've ever had."

Dad wasn't stupid. His son was a typical service brat. He had never been anywhere long enough to make firm friends, moving every two years with his father's new postings. Also, Harry had noticed that his son had no female friends and had never had a date. The word made him cringe, but he was pretty sure Phill was a faggot.

"Alright, Phill, if he's that important to you, I'll talk to the headmaster and see if he will allow it."

"Thanks Dad, you're the best."

It was only a few days later that both boys were summoned to the headmaster's study.

"Mr. Calalang, Mr. Affleck's father has asked that you be allowed to stay with him and his son during the mid-term break. If you both wish that to happen, I have no objection."

Both boys grinned and replied as though it was rehearsed, "Oh, yes please, Sir."

"Very well, Major Affleck has said he will pick you up and sign the necessary forms at the same time. That's all."

Both boys almost bounced out of the head's study.

"I love you Filipino boy, and for a whole week I'm going to have you in my bed and show you."

That was said with a totally lecherous look on his face reducing Sam to tears of laughter. When he could speak, Sam replied in a very high voice.

"Oh, you wicked man, you want to defile my body and take my virginity," then he lowered his voice to normal and finished with, "I hope."

Too much—both boys had to cling together for support—they were laughing so hard. When they were calmed down again, Phill looked at Sam and told him how it was.

"I love you Sam, and I want to spend a lot of time kissing you and cuddling you while I tell you how happy you make me. I do want to explore sex with you, but mostly I want to be able to show you how I feel."

Sam was surprised at how intense Phill sounded.

"I guess I feel the same, it's quite a while since anyone made me feel loved. We have nearly a year Phill, we don't have to go mad. I'd like to take time to see what we both like."

Phill nodded his agreement and they continued to class on a high from the knowledge they had just obtained.

Chapter 2

The boys were picked up in a United States Air Force staff car, driven by Phill's dad in uniform. He looked very imposing, and Sam felt very small when he was introduced even though he equalled the Major in stature.

"I'm very pleased to meet you, Sir, and thank you for letting me stay with you."

He dropped his eyes then and looked at the Major's shoes. Harry looked at his son and smiled. He could see the happiness in those eyes that he had seen sadness in far too often.

"You are very welcome, Sam. Now, let's get your bags in the car."

He moved to his son and gave him a hug.

"Look after your friend, Son, while I see the headmaster."

When Harry came out of the school again, he noticed a crowd of boys stood round looking at the car. He hopped in and noticed both boys in the back. Laughing, he told them:

"Even generals don't have majors as their driver, so make the most of this one."

He could see as he drove off how close the boys sat to each other and how happy they both were—almost confirming his thoughts. It made him sad because he knew there was no chance these boys would ever be able to show their true feelings for each other in any public environment.

It only took Harry a couple of days to realise that his son had picked a winner. Sam was the model of good manners and helpfulness. Nothing appeared to be too much trouble. He was clean and tidy as well, which scored points with a military man. He started to wonder then what would happen to him when he finished school. By then, Harry would probably be on his way back to the States, putting Phill into college somewhere. If this relationship blossomed, could he persuade the American authorities to let him adopt the boy, giving him a second son? He would almost certainly make half colonel after this appointment, so funding a second son wouldn't be a problem if the authorities didn't help.

Meanwhile, Phill and Sam had taken advantage of their daily alone time to explore each other's bodies. The first morning after Harry left for work was the benchmark for the next week.

"Back to bed, Sam, I want us to find out how far we want to go with sex. I loved cuddling you last night but we had pyjamas on. Now I want us to start the same way, only naked."

They stood by the bed and slowly stripped. Phill was almost panting as Sam got down to underpants. He had never seen him completely naked, able to look instead of just take a quick glance, and he could see already that Sam was monumentally erect. When the pants came off, Phill gasped. Sam's cock was very thick and about 8 inches long. He was pleased that he could top that in length, but nowhere near in thickness. Sam's body was superb as well, he was very buff.

"Oh, Sam, I think I may disgrace myself when I start touching you. Your body is fantastic, and that cock is going to occupy an awful lot of my time."

Sam was delighted. He felt the same way about Phill, having already seen him naked and erect. Now he was almost panting at the thought of being able to touch it.

They fell onto the bed and nose to nose, toes to toes, started kissing. They used their free arm to pull their bodies even closer together so that both could feel their hard cocks touching and pressed into their tummies.

"I love you Phill, I never expected to be this happy after my initial reception at the school. It has been a very lonely year, but now I have you and I have never been happier."

While they were kissing, they started stroking each other's bodies. When Sam got to Phill's butt, he teared up.

"That feels so good… I know that one day I want to put my cock in there, but will you fuck me first? I want to give myself to you with love, the way I saw boys give themselves to American G.I.s after they freed us."

Phill pulled back then.

"You mean our soldiers used to fuck boys?"

"Oh yes," Sam replied. "They were always taking them off to private places. When they came back, the boys would have bars of chocolate and packs of cigarettes. They could make lots of money on selling them."

"Did you do it as well, Sam?"

"Oh no, I am still a virgin. That is why I want you to fuck me. I love you Phill, it is only right that you should be the one to take that virginity."

Phill was overcome. Sam obviously took the loss of his virginity seriously. He realised that he wanted the same thing, but Sam was very thick. He was sure it would hurt immensely when he tried to push that into him.

"I feel the same way, Sam, but you are so thick. My little hole will never take it I am sure."

Sam laughed. "Oh you will be fine. My friends told me how the G.I.s opened them up with spit slicked fingers, and then they used Vaseline on their cocks and poked some up inside the boy. They said it made entry very easy. It was only the ones that went in dry that upset them and sometimes made them bleed."

Phill couldn't imagine giving up his virginity for anything except love, but then, he hadn't been in a war ravaged country.

"Well, neither of us is going that far today because we have no Vaseline."

Sam grinned. "Oh good, I just want to spend lots of time playing with you and making your cock spit."

Both boys laughed but then pulled apart far enough to be able to play with each other. Sam teared up after he had felt all round Phill's groin and then started gently jacking him.

"What's wrong Sam, what have I done to upset you?"

"Oh nothing, nothing at all. I am just so happy. I have wanted to do this since the first time I saw you naked. I wanted to take your cock in my mouth and lick it all up."

Phill was wide-eyed as he replied. "Well you can, that sounds so exciting."

Sam swivelled round, and holding Phill's cock steady with one hand, he started licking the head before moving down it and licking the balls as well. This was the stuff of dreams. He wondered how he could be so lucky. This American boy was just amazing.

"Mmmm, Sam, I think I could let you do that all day."

"Oh good, because I want to see how much you cum the first time, and then I want to taste it."

For Phill, this was getting better by the minute, so he moved round a little more to do the same to Sam. Up close and licking made Phill realise how fantastic Sam's appendage was. It was so thick it was like having a large lollipop to lick on, only much more exciting.

Conversation ceased then as both boys went on a voyage of discovery. On their sides, with the upper leg bent, left their butts open for exploration as well. Sam was in his element. He was happily sucking Phill's cock while using his free hand to stroke his butt and run a finger down the crack to impact the anus. Phill gasped—it was so sensitive. Running his finger over the entry for a few minutes and Sam had an unintended mouthful of cum. He swallowed it, not knowing what else to do. He realised it tasted fine so he kept sucking Phill gently, while Phill brought Sam to orgasm as well. He didn't feel brave enough to swallow it so he let it all spray out on to Sam's belly.

"Oh crikey, Sam, I'm sorry I didn't swallow yours."

Sam laughed. "That's okay. I loved the taste of yours, so I don't mind."

Phill hopped out of bed, grabbed a towel and cleaned up Sam's tummy before hopping back into bed and cuddling him.

"That was fantastic, I nearly stopped breathing when you touched my anus. I think when it is your cock and not your finger, I will never stop cumming."

"Oh, I hope so, then I will take lots of time to lick it all off your body."

"I'll do the same to you next time, Sam."

"You don't have to. I don't suppose we will both like the same thing to the same degree. I think the important thing is that we find what we both enjoy and make sure we please our partner."

Phill was so pleased that Sam felt like that. He thought it was very adult.

"Let's go and explore the village before lunch, and then come back to bed for a while before dad gets home."

"Yes please, and we can buy a pot of Vaseline as well."

Sam was grinning as he said that. *'Maybe we'll use it tomorrow',* was Sam's thought, mirrored by Phill.

The village in Suffolk was so quaint to Phill's eyes; like something out of a story book. To Sam it was just the prettiest sight he had ever seen. They called in at a little general store and picked up a few bits for the food store at home that didn't require food stamps, and a little jar of Vaseline at the chemists. Phill appeared to have loads of money and Sam felt guilty that he had none at all. No one had thought about pocket money for this refugee boy. He was clothed, fed and educated; no one thought he should have anything else. Phill picked up on it and blushed when he realised Sam was embarrassed.

"Oh Sam, I'm sorry, I know you don't have any money. Please don't be upset, you are my best friend in the whole world, and dad is very generous with my allowance so it doesn't matter that you have no money. We are partners and lovers so what is mine is yours."

Sam's turn to blush and then almost whisper.

"I'm not always going to be poor, Phill. One day, I promise I will pay you back everything."

Phill laughed then as he replied.

"I'm going to hold you to that. You are going to be my lover until you have paid me back everything, so I have you until we finish college and then for years afterwards."

That was another source of worry for Sam. How was he going to be able to go to college? Phill guessed what the worried look was about.

"We are going to be together Sam, no matter what. Dad will almost certainly send me back to the States to go to college after this year. I will dig my heels in and refuse to go unless you go with me."

Sam was shocked at that comment. He never expected that kind of commitment from this American boy.

"You'll never be able to make that happen. The Brits will almost certainly send me back to the Philippines when I finish school. I am already eighteen, which makes me an adult in my country."

That gave Phill food for thought, and the thought was, *'Twenty one is the legal age of adulthood so perhaps dad could adopt Sam.'*

When they got back to the house, all thoughts about the future disappeared as they dumped their shopping and went up to Phill's bedroom to get undressed and start another love in. The kissing and caressing were getting extremely heated as each boy discovered the most sensitive areas on their lover. For Sam, it was definitely Phill's cock. He could almost orgasm just thinking about it sliding over his sphincter and burying itself in his bottom. Phill was greedy. He loved playing with Sam's incredible cock—but he really wanted to fuck him. No problem with these two on that score, even without voicing their preferences. Sam made it abundantly clear by the way he positioned his legs that he wanted Phill to explore his arse. The first slicked up finger to penetrate him made him gasp.

"Oh yes, Phill, that feels amazing, please keep doing it."

Phill was grinning like an idiot, he was so thrilled watching his finger slide in and out of Sam's cute butt. He added a second one, and then with a little Vaseline on the fingers, a third one. He fucked Sam with the three for a few minutes while he continued to suck on his cock and play with his balls. Sam was so turned on, he came off Phill's cock and gasped out a message for Phill:

"Please Phil, put your cock in me. I want you to take my virginity *now*."

Phill rolled Sam on to his back and got between his legs. Without being told, Sam parted his legs very wide and bent them up and away from Phill giving him unimpeded access to his butt. Phill coated his cock with Vaseline and placed it at the entrance to Sam's anus.

"Are you sure Babe? Really sure, you want me to do this?"

Sam had tears in his eyes as he replied.

"Yes please, I want this more than anything else in the world. I love you Phill, it's only right you should take my virginity."

A little pressure and Phill's cock head slid over Sam's sphincter to a sigh of contentment.

"That feels amazing, give me all of you."

Phill continued the penetration until he hit the second barrier, when he stopped, having seen the spike of pain in Sam's eyes, and felt the resistance.

"It's okay Phill, you can keep going."

Phill didn't understand, but he did as Sam asked until he was fully inserted. He fell forward and kissed Sam, passionately.

"You have all of me Sam. Is that ok?"

Sam grinned. "Oh God, yes. It feels amazing. Fuck me now, plant your seed in me and make me yours forever."

Phill started crying tears of happiness as he very gently slow fucked Sam to an incredible orgasm, playing with him all the time as well, so that they came almost together in the most intense orgasm either had ever experienced. Phill could hardly take his eyes off Sam's butt as he watched his cock pistoning in and out of it, and Sam was mesmerised by the look on Phill's face, showing the emotions he was experiencing.

Sometime later, two very happy boys were almost hysterical as they finally pulled apart and looked at the mess of Sam's cum spread across their chests and tummies. Phill knelt back and took hold of Sam's balls.

"Wow, you still have them. It looks as though you emptied them in one go when we orgasmed."

Sam giggled like a little girl. He was so happy and Phill made it better by making it fun.

"I think we should have a bath before dad comes home and sees us like this."

No dissent there and two very happy boys were in the kitchen raiding the pantry in no time, having worked up an appetite with the sex.

When Harry arrived home, the boys were in the lounge reading and listening to the radio. When they looked up to greet him, he knew instantly that something in their lives had changed. The looks of complete happiness on their faces left no room for doubt. He guessed that these two had consummated their love. It gave him much food for thought during the evening as he confirmed his first impression of the boys' feelings for one another. They talked about their day and the missing hours spent in bed were noted by Harry without comment.

Nothing changed with the boys for their week off. Harry saw how the love they had for each other grew and almost consumed them. On the last day, he sat them down to talk to them before returning them to their school.

"You both know that the relationship you have is totally taboo both sides of the Atlantic, don't you?"

Heads dropped and they mumbled a reply.

"Yes Dad." And "Yes Sir."

"Well in that case, you must know that your eyes give you away every time you look at each other. When you get back to school, please be careful or you are going to give yourself away. Try to strike up friendships with other boys so that it is less obvious that you love each other."

Phill looked up at his dad almost in shock.

"What do you mean love, Dad?"

"Come on son. I'm not stupid. You both almost shout it with your eyes."

Phill collapsed then, crying his eyes out.

"I love Sam so much, Dad. How are we going to stay together when we finish school? I'm so frightened that I'm going to lose him."

Harry knew then that he had a mountain to climb to keep these boys together.

"I can't promise you anything concrete, Phill, but I will promise you I'll try to organise it so that you go to college together."

Phill stopped crying immediately and looked deep into his father's eyes.

"Do you mean that, Dad? Really mean it?"

Harry nodded, "If your love remains strong, I will do everything I can to keep you together after you graduate from school."

Two very happy boys returned to school the next day.

Chapter 3

A serious boy watcher would have been in hysterics if he could have seen Phill and Sam attempting to broaden their friends' base. They could seriously have achieved it if they had really wanted to, but they always appeared to gravitate back to one another after only short spells. Winter gave way to spring, and soccer gave way to athletics. Both boys were good enough to represent the school and their team mates liked them, but it became obvious as the term wore on that they were quite content in each other's company and didn't need any one else.

Robbie McCormack was the first one to actually mention it because he had a very acute "gaydar." He was also a very self-confidant young man and not too worried about using people to get what he wanted. A little before end of term, he decided to act on his suspicions.

"Hi there. Can I join you for a few minutes?"

Phill looked round. The recreation room was almost empty, there were plenty of free chairs and Robbie was not one of their friends.

"Sure Robbie, but to what do we owe this visit?"

Robbie grinned.

"I just want to tell you something that I have discovered by close observation of you since we came back at half term. You two are homosexuals."

He sat back then, looking very smug and watching their faces. Sam was a dead giveaway with his shocked expression. Phill was much more composed.

"I have never heard such rubbish. If that is the best you can do, I suggest you fuck off."

"Good try Affleck, but your lover gave you away."

Phill looked at Sam and his heart sank. Sam was looking terrified.

"Alright Robbie, just supposing you are correct. We would both deny it and just say that as the only two aliens in this class, we have bonded and became good friends. I don't think you'll be able to prove anything else."

"Probably not, but even the rumour would make your last term pretty miserable, and if you did slip up even once, someone would be bound to see and you would be off to prison."

Sam gasped and ran from the room.

"I'll talk to you again later Robbie, after supper."

Then Phill ran after Sam, and found him in one of the toilets cowering in a cubicle and crying his eyes out.

Phill took his lover in his arms and stroked his back as he talked to him.

"It's okay Babe, nothing is going to happen. If he wanted to out us to the authorities, he would have done so. He is going to ask for something to keep his mouth shut. I'm sure we can sort it out."

Sam slowly calmed down and looked at his soul mate.

"Do you really think so?"

"Yes my love, I'm sure of it. I'll sort it out after supper."

"I love you so much, Phill, I'll run away rather than let them hurt you."

Phill was shocked at that.

"Don't you dare, I'll never forgive you if you leave me. We'll sort this together, do you understand?"

Sam knew then that he had to go along with whatever Phill wanted.

He nodded, and said, "But I'm so frightened."

Phill teared up a little as well.

"So am I, but we have to brave this through if we want a future together."

After supper, they went for a walk with Robbie.

"Okay, assuming you are correct about Sam and me, what do you want to keep your mouth shut?"

"I want you to come to my house after church on Sunday and be my slaves for a few hours."

Phill was confused. "What do you mean your house?"

"I live locally but my parents are so seldom there that they made me a boarder. They are away at the moment so I have the run of an empty house."

"Alright, Robbie, and what do you mean be your slaves?"

"I want to use your bodies the same as I could do if you were real slaves."

"Doing what?"

"That's entirely up to me. You will do anything I ask."

"And how often would you want us to perform for you?"

"I'm not sure. That would depend on how this first session went."

Phill knew he had limited bargaining power but he was going to do his best.

"We will be the best slaves you could possibly wish for but these are our conditions. It only happens once, and you don't do anything that leaves us incapacitated or marked."

Robbie didn't like that.

"Not acceptable, at least once per month until the end of the school year."

Phill thought, it was now March, so four months before the end of the school year.

"That's four months. I'll agree three sessions and that's the limit, and only then if you don't do anything disgusting to us."

Robbie could see the steel in Phill's look and thought he was probably not going to get any better.

"What do you mean disgusting?"

Phill shrugged, "I don't know. You tell us now what you are going to do and I'll tell you if I'm going to allow it."

"Okay, I'm going to fuck you both, make you give me blowjobs and fuck each other as well. If you are not enthusiastic, I will punish you like they do at school, only you will be naked for it."

"I'm not sure I'm going to allow you to touch Sam, but what if I up the visits to five and only me?"

Sam had been listening and jumped in.

"You said we do this together Phill. I don't mind if he fucks me. Loads of my friends did it in Manila after the war and it didn't worry them. It's only sex, and as long as he doesn't damage me for you, I'm going to be okay with it."

Robbie was really surprised then to see Phill pull Sam into a hug and a serious kiss before saying. "I love you so much Sam, I'll kill him if he hurts you."

Then he turned to Robbie again.

"Okay, we'll do it, but if you ever breathe a word of this to anyone else, I'll make you eternally sorry, even if it puts me in prison."

Robbie replied, "Okay I'll see you in the quad after church on Sunday. I'll supply lunch and have you back here before curfew." Then he fled.

Robbie's mind was in turmoil. He had no idea that homosexuals fell in love like ordinary people. He thought how wonderful it would be to get into a relationship like Sam and Phill had.

After church on Sunday, Phill, with his jar of Vaseline (just in case) and Sam, grabbed bicycles with Robbie and cycled to his house about fifteen minutes away.

The house was a detached one and obviously in quite a good area. Inside it was very plush, and Robbie's bedroom where they ended up was large with a big bed and a sitting area with a small coffee table and an armchair.

"Alright you two. Until we leave here, you do everything I tell you without question, you address me as Sir and you take up the positions I tell you, immediately I tell you. Do you understand?"

Phill looked at him pityingly. "What's not to understand?"

"Sir."

Phill tried to stare him down but capitulated in the end, "Sir."

"Good. I will punish you for that little attempted rebellion, but not just yet. To start with, I want you both stripped naked."

Robbie was almost salivating when he saw these two sexy boys standing naked in front of him.

"Now when I say 'display,' you will stand with your legs well spread and your hands clasped behind your head. When I say 'spread,' you will take up the display position and then bend over and use your hands to spread your arse cheeks as wide as you can for me to inspect your arseholes. Fuck 1 is on the bed on your back, legs well spread and pulled back so that the knees are level with your shoulders. Fuck 2 is on all fours but with your head on your arms, legs well spread. Punishment will be any position I detail."

Robbie ran through them almost cumming at the spread position. Seeing two well displayed anuses was so erotic for him.

"That was very good. Now display, I'm going to play with you."

Robbie was almost crying with pleasure when he stood back and looked at two very hard cocks.

"Very impressive. Now I want you both on the bed and you are to make love. This first time, I want you Sam to fuck Phill. I'm sure he will love to feel that fat monster in his arse."

Phill got the Vaseline from his jacket pocket and put it on the bedside table. Robbie looked at it not knowing why they had it, but said nothing.

It took Sam almost half an hour to make love to Phill, giving Robbie an amazing display of loving sex. After they had both orgasmed, Sam fell forward onto Phill's chest and Robbie heard him quite clearly.

"I love you so much, you are my life, now and always."

The kiss that followed made Robbie's toes curl, and he wasn't even receiving it. He burst into tears then, shocking the other two.

"I'm so sorry," he sobbed, "I didn't know you loved each other. Please forgive me. I don't want to abuse you now that I know. Please Phill. Will you punish me and then use my body to show me how evil I have been?"

Sam and Phil were rendered speechless, but Sam got off the bed and squatted down beside Robbie, took him in his arms and quietly spoke to him.

"It's okay Robbie, no harm has been done. We understand. Please don't cry."

Robbie looked at him and then at Phill.

"But you must hate me for what I have done."

Phill jumped in then.

"What have you done? Let me see. You've played with us and got us lovely erections. You made Sam make love to me which I love almost as much as I love making love to him. So what is evil about anything you have done?"

Robbie looked at these two class mates as though they were mad.

"But I had wicked intent until I saw how much you love each other."

"Yes, you did, that's true."

Turning to Sam, he whispered. "Would you mind if we have a little fun with Robbie and make him feel better? It will involve some sex."

Sam thought this might be interesting so he grinned and told his lover to do what he liked.

"Okay Robbie. Confirm, you are homosexual as well."

Robbie nodded.

"Also, that you are an anal virgin."

Again Robbie nodded.

"Very well then. You will be our slave now. Do you agree, as payment for your evil deed?"

Again Robbie nodded. He was getting good at it.

"Okay, stand up and strip naked. Then play with yourself and get an erection."

Sam and Phill stood back and watched as Robbie, very self-consciously stripped naked. He played with himself finishing with a neat six incher.

"Now turn around and spread."

Sam and Phill looked at each other then and Phill whispered.

"Are you okay with both of us making love to him now and finishing with me fucking him and you getting a blowjob?"

Sam nodded, thinking that would be a first for him: sex with someone other than Phill.

They positioned Robbie on his bed with the two of them either side of him. They took their time exploring his body, working from head to toe on each side. Attacking Robbie's groin was fun because they kept getting in each other's way and used that as an excuse for a few kisses. Robbie missed nothing and realised even more how much these two classmates loved each other, and more surprisingly found this sex act fun. They weren't at all embarrassed sucking a cock and balls watching each other. By the time both of them were reaching overload pleasuring this sexy friend, they moved end to end and Phill started opening Robbie's anus, while Sam continued kissing him and exciting his nipples. All three boys were gasping when Phill slid his cockhead over Robbie's sphincter and Sam entered his mouth. A thorough spit-roasting with both boys attacking Robbie's cock and balls, all the time, soon had three very intense orgasms occur at almost the same time. All three boys thought how incredibly erotic it was, and fell in a jumbled heap afterwards while they recovered.

"Now let that be a lesson to you." Phill said, with a huge grin on his face.

Robbie was still in a daze at how incredible this first proper gay sex had been.

"I think I love you guys. Can I be your slave again sometime?"

Much laughter until Phill got serious.

"What do you think, Lover? Shall we continue his education occasionally?"

Sam could see that Phill wouldn't have a problem with that, so he replied:

"Mmm, I think that might be a good idea, but don't you think we should punish him first for attempting to mischief make?"

So they did. They turned Robbie over and each of them plastered his bottom with about twenty slaps. The lovely tingle they set up was what they intended. Afterwards they made him sit up on his knees and Phill stroked his bottom while Sam gave him a blowjob. Robbie couldn't believe how sensuous all that was, his orgasm being testament to his enjoyment.

All calmed down, bathed and dressed again, Robbie talked to the other two.

"I'm sorry I contemplated being evil to you two, but I'm pleased I did. The sex we just had was absolutely amazing. If you would like to do that again, any time, I will be delighted."

Three very contented young men returned to school for supper that Sunday, and another friendship was born.

Chapter 4

End of term and the boys went home for Easter. Nothing had changed at home and they had two weeks of loving. Harry was now well aware of the level of arousal that they induced in each other. The love they had for each other just filled the house with an aura. He realised that he would have to make a huge effort to keep them together. He contacted the American Embassy in London and stated his case to adopt a Filipino boy and send him back to the States with his biological son.

"The boy is a refugee, brought here by the British Government and placed in a private school. They will probably send him back to the Philippines at the end of the school year, so I don't see them giving us any trouble if we get him a student visa for home."

The embassy contact was also ex-military, having mustered out at the end of the war, and so he was sympathetic towards Sam's situation.

"Major, you may have hit the nail on the head. We can get him a student visa, no problem, if you guarantee him financially. I can probably get him a free scholarship as well provided his stats are good. Once he is in the States you can take your time over adoption to keep him there after he finishes his degree."

Harry was over the moon and was very exuberant in his thanks—making the embassy guy curious.

"Why the enthusiasm, Major?"

Alarm bells ringing.

"My son and this boy have become very good friends. Both aliens here, and in the case of Sam, no family."

The embassy official was gay and thought these two boys might be as well.

"Bring them down to London and ask for me. Make sure they have their passports and two extra photos. Also, let me have their school stats up to date."

Time and date arranged, Harry grabbed the boys and took them into his base to get the photos; rang the headmaster at their school, explained the situation and stats were put in the post.

The boys were mesmerised by the war damage done to this great city as Harry drove them to the American Embassy. Tom Ryan met them in reception and took them to his office. He looked through the paperwork and breathed a sigh of relief. The boys were both academically sound, so Sam's student visa would not be a problem. Their love for each other, if you were looking for it, just screamed at you.

"Major, I'd like to talk to the boys in private for a few minutes, and then if you take them out to lunch I should have a list of colleges that will take Sam on scholarship. You will then be able to get your son into the same one."

Harry was happy with that and sat with a coffee in the embassy café until the boys joined him.

"Sam and Phill. The reason for this private session is that I am 100% convinced you two are lovers."

Both boys saw their hopes shattered and burst into tears as they hugged each other.

Tom was surprised and pleased for them. He knew that they would almost certainly never be able to express their love for one another in public, but he didn't think they would worry if they had each other. He moved from his desk and hugged the boys, speaking softly.

"Be good for one another and be careful with your love. There are a lot of people out there who will try to destroy it if they know. I will recommend colleges that are considered liberal so that you won't have too much trouble even if your relationship is suspected."

Sam and Phill looked at this man that held the key to their happiness. Phill was the first to speak.

"Why would you do that, now that you know we are faggots?"

"Because the love of my life was killed at Iwo Jima, and I don't think I will ever find anyone to replace him. I will help you all I can in memory of him."

Poor Tom. The boys almost buried him in kisses. Back behind his desk, eventually he spoke again.

"I will be back in the States in three years' time and I hope then to become an assistant professor. If it's at the same college as you two, I might let you do that again."

All three were laughing as Tom showed them out of his office. The boys were so happy when they re-joined Harry that he guessed the talk had been positive.

The after lunch meeting with Tom Ryan had both boys goggle eyed.

"My old college in California will take both these boys, Major. Sam will go on a full scholarship as a refugee, and Phill will get a full scholarship as the son of a serving officer. They will be expected at the beginning of the next academic year and all of their joining details will be sent to your address in Suffolk. If you need any help with the British authorities, just let me know and I will do everything I can to help."

Harry was more than a little surprised when they said goodbye. The boys gave Tom a kiss on the lips and a hug. He didn't say anything, guessing that the boys had found a kindred spirit. He got the story on the drive home.

The British authorities were delighted to get rid of responsibility for Sam. The economy was on its knees after a terrible war, so Sam was to be released into Harry's care at the end of the school year.

Both boys decided they would take Robbie to bed one more time before leaving the school, and they would allow him to be the slave master and fuck both of them if he wanted to. Neither of them could believe the buckets of tears that Robbie shed after he had made love to them both.

"I know I will never experience anything nearly as erotic and wonderful as this again if I live to be a hundred. I love you guys. Please stay in touch when you get back to America."

"Of course we will," Phill said, "You'll be our first gay pen pal, and if you ever make it to California, or wherever else we are, you can be our fuck buddy as well."

Phil looked at Sam for confirmation of that last statement.

"Oh yes, Robbie has such an exciting body, and he fucks pretty well too."

All three dissolved in laughter after that comment.

Chapter 5

The Military transport from Suffolk flew the boys to Edwards Air Force Base first. They were met by a liaison officer who saw them onwards to California with their college joining instructions. Their information packs showed that their bank accounts were already set up for them and Sam was told his would be topped up to a certain level every semester that he remained at college. Phill already knew that his father would keep his topped up as well.

"There is an initial lump sum that the State has decided you should have for clothes and college equipment Mr. Calalang, on top of your allowance."

Sam was delighted. He couldn't believe that so many good things were happening thanks to Phill's father and their contact, Tom Ryan. The rolling campus, the hundreds of students from many nations, all of it just took his breath away. The icing on the cake for them was a two-man dorm. They had to share a bathroom with the whole floor but, so what. They realised that they would have to plan their sex. Wet washcloths would need to be at the ready for afterwards so that they weren't covered in cum when they went for showers.

They settled in with ease, making friends quickly. They both had such interesting stories to tell that they were almost mobbed in the student lounges. Sam was probably the happiest student on campus, and being such a beautiful boy as well, it didn't take him and Phill long to gather round them a coterie of other gay young men. No one was actually "out," but they soon developed a secret handshake which always brought peals of laughter to their meeting. Being able to relax a little with their love was so good for the boys' psyche. The only thing that really set them apart from their peers was that they seldom partied and never indulged in the new craze of smoking marijuana.

Harry had been true to his word. When he was posted back to the States a year after the boys, he took the necessary steps and completed adoption of Sam before his 21st birthday. Sam's new name was Sam Ciriaco Affleck.

"I know it sounds odd, Sir, but I would like my old name to remind me of my roots."

Harry laughed. "That's okay, Sam. The only name that matters to the authorities is your last one."

Sam was so proud the first time he saw his new name on an official document. He cried with pleasure and had that added to by Harry telling him he could now call him 'Dad' or 'Harry,' whatever he liked. Despite being nearly 20 years old, Sam looked very shy as he replied.

"I'd like to call you, Dad."

Deed done and after their vacation both boys returned to college and Harry to duty, also in California. Now promoted half colonel, he was a happy man.

At the beginning of their third year both boys were surprised to see an invitation in their mail boxes to a soiree to welcome a new assistant professor to the college. It was a staff party and no explanation was forthcoming as to why two ordinary students should be invited. They soon found out when they entered the Dean's house showing their invitations. It looked very intimidating. There were loads of faculty with their significant other halves, but no other students. The dean approached them as they looked round and smiling, offered his hand.

"You two must have made quite an impression on our new colleague. I have never had a new member of staff request students at his welcome party. Let me take you to reacquaint Professor Ryan with you."

Sam and Phill knew then and were delighted to see a grinning Tom as they approached him.

"It is so good to see you two again. The Dean has told me that you have done me proud with both your academic and athletic performance."

Both boys blushed which pleased the dean. A little modesty in students was an unusual characteristic.

"I will leave you to get re-acquainted. We will officially welcome you here Tom, when all the guests have arrived."

It was quite obvious instantly that Tom was very taken with both boys who had another two years of maturity to show.

"You two are even more devastating than when I saw you at the embassy. I presume life has been good to you and your love has grown."

Ever the extrovert, Phill replied.

"Yes, Sir, and we owe you for that. We would never have got this without your whole hearted support for us. We both owe you more than we can ever repay you. Sam is now Sam Affleck as well so he will be able to remain in the States forever."

"I am more than delighted Phill, and I would very much like you to call me Tom when we aren't with other faculty, or in lectures."

"I'd like that, Tom," was Phill's reply, and a very shy Sam replied, "Thank you, Sir."

Lots of laughter then and the party was definitely a feather in the cap for the two boys. Faculty wouldn't forget them in a hurry, which in their cases, as serious students always benefited them.

Tom didn't have any lectures with the boys, but they did get invitations to his rooms for soirees with other students. It wasn't long before they realised that Tom had gathered round him several other gay students. He admitted to them one day that he had a quite acute gaydar.

"Even when they aren't in relationships like you two, I can often souse them out. If they are a couple it is even easier, like it was with you two."

Their friendship grew to the pleasure of Sam and Phill. Tom as friend and mentor, always ready to help them. With the summer athletics programme in full swing the boys were surprised to see Tom in the changing rooms with them one day.

"You are all putting me to shame so I have started running again, and the field coach thinks I am good enough to run middle distance, so here I am in training."

When they showered afterwards they had the opportunity to scope out each other, and weren't slow to do just that.

Tom disgraced himself quickly, but only the boys saw it. He developed an erection looking at the boys.

"God, you two are even more devastating than I imagined."

Sam grew another inch taller at that compliment and Phill grinned before making the obvious comment.

"You aren't exactly chopped liver yourself, Tom. That body is phenomenal. Abs and pecs to die for, and little Tom looks as hard as iron. Very impressive."

Phill's comment only told the half of it. Tom was in perfect shape, good strong legs to run on, broad powerful shoulders and sat on top was a strong face with startling blue eyes, topped with a head of rich brown hair. The whole was coated in a light fuzz of dark hair making it look incredibly sexy to both boys.

"He may not be the biggest in the world, but what he lacks in size he makes up for in ability."

The boys agreed that it looked hard enough to wreak havoc with a welcoming anus.

"Six inches of nuclear power."

Tom laughed as he said it and the boys looked at each other with mixed emotions. Later they talked about it and agreed that they had done it with Robbie and enjoyed it, so perhaps, if Tom asked, they might enjoy it with him.

The chance to find out wasn't long in coming. Tom invited them to his room for drinks one evening. When they arrived they were the only two guests.

"Just us three tonight because I want to have a serious talk with you both."

Quizzical looks and Tom continued.

"When I first saw you two in my office in London, I knew you were gay and my little Tom let me know that I thought you were both incredibly sexy. Seeing you again here was even more convincing for me. You have both matured into the most amazingly sexy young men. You said when we first talked here that you would never be able to repay me for what I had done for you both. Would you be prepared to try if I put something to you?"

Neither boy could think where this was going so replied in the affirmative.

"We would do anything to please you Tom. We told you when you came here what you have done for us."

Tom looked embarrassed but forged ahead.

"Okay, well, I would like to take you both to bed."

If they hadn't already been sat down, both boys would almost certainly have fallen down. They gulped, Phill looked at Sam who just shrugged and then nodded.

"Would you like to expand on that, Tom?"

"Ok, I have lusted after you two for two years. Now that I have seen you naked, that lust has grown a thousand fold and I want to feel your two cocks reaming out my ass, and mine reaming out yours. I'm a swinger, happy to top or bottom and you two are the source of wet dreams for me."

Tom laughed to hide his embarrassment at his admission.

Sam took the lead then—why he, couldn't have told you, because he nearly always left decisions to Phill.

"I'm 8 ½ by 6 ½, Tom, but if you think you can take it, I would love to feel your lips surround it at either end."

Phill laughed and jumped in as well.

"Count me in on that, Tom, you are a bloody sexy guy, and that rod of iron hammering my prostate some time will, I am sure, have me serial orgasming."

Tom couldn't believe how easy that was.

"Do you two play around a lot then?"

They laughed and told him about Robbie, at school.

"Neither of us has done anything since, but we talked about doing it with you after athletics last week."

Three grinning young men had a drink and talked about the when. A Sunday was agreed starting after lunch.

Chapter 6

Phill and Sam were almost panting with anticipation as they made their way to Tom's room after lunch on Sunday. He greeted them both with kisses and then offered them drinks. Over the drinks he told them his idea.

"I know you two must be incredibly experienced together, so why don't we start this by you two being the leaders and bossing me around. I'll commit to doing anything you tell me for a couple of hours, and then I want to take charge of you two. I have plenty of lubricant on the bedside cabinet. I'm a long way from being a virgin so you don't need to treat me like rare porcelain. In fact if you want to be a little rough I won't mind, and that includes CP if you feel like it. I don't indulge in that very often but I certainly did at school. I'm sure half of my masters were sadists or paedophiles, or both."

"I can imagine that, Tom, if I had been a master when you were a teenager I would probably have had you across my knees frequently. You are bloody sexy now, I can't imagine what you were like then."

Phill blushed a little after that statement but Tom laughed and told him he was pleased with the comment.

Tom was 28. He had graduated college at 21, done two years in the navy and left to join the State Department while he did his doctorate part time. His college had offered him an assistant professor job when he got his doctorate. One of the fun parts of this job was that he looked like one of the undergraduates and played on it until people found out the truth. He had a bevy of young, beautiful, gay men that he called "friend", but these two were the ones he truly lusted after.

"Ok, shall we begin? I'm yours to command, my beautiful friends."

"I want you to strip just where you are, Tom. I'm going to get a good feel of your body."

By the time Tom was naked, he was also erect.

"Spread your legs, Tom."

With that done, Phill walked round the back and started stroking Tom from shoulders to knees. Sam stood at the front looking a little embarrassed, but he took Tom's cock in his hand to stroke it.

"Oh my God, Phill. You have to feel this. I have never felt a cock this hard. It really is like a rod of steel. That has to be the most incredible fuck stick. I bet Tom can use it like a guided missile."

Tom grinned.

"I'll let you find out later."

Phill came round the front to feel it as well.

"Oh wow, I'm impressed, Tom. We can attack both ends together Sam, after he has worked his magic on us. I think you should strip us now, Tom, and have a little play with both of us to give us an idea of your ability before you give us both blowjobs."

Tom loved this, particularly when he had got them both naked and hard. He wanted to cry with pleasure when he saw the two erect cocks—they were amazing. Both longer than his own and in the case of Sam, almost intimidating. He was playing with Sam's cock and balls when he spoke.

"Are you the top or the bottom Sam?"

Sam smiled, "I am whatever mood Phill is in. I love him inside me, but when he wants to be passive I love to feel my little brain being caressed by Phill's insides."

"Brave man Phill, I think I will need a lot of opening up before I can take that."

"You'll love it when you do, Tom. It is quite addictive."

This was all settling down nicely so Phill told Sam to sit and let Tom give him a blowjob.

"I'm sure you will need the nutrition so I expect you to swallow all his sperm, Tom."

Grinning like an idiot, Tom replied.

"Of course, I'm not going to waste anything this boy wants to give me."

Phill sat and watched as Tom made love to Sam's cock and balls. He was watching a real master. Tom's experience showed and very quickly he had Sam wriggling like an eel.

"Oh God, Phill, you have to feel this. I think Tom is a magician."

Phill watched. When Tom was attacking Sam's balls, he held his hand behind them and licked very hard so that he pushed the balls back into the palm of his hand. After a minute or two he would use the same pressure as he licked up Sam's cock as it lay against his stomach. Then at the top he would lift it and gently lick round the head before taking it in his mouth and swabbing it. While he was doing that, the other hand was continuing to play with the balls, occasionally sliding to the perineum and stroking that. A few more minutes of play and then Tom swallowed all of Sam's cock and started massaging it with his throat. Sam was about to cum, and Tom just pulled off and stroked Sam's body, giving him time to calm down before starting all over again. Each time he brought Sam close to orgasm, the sensation was more acute until Tom gaged it just right: when it would have been almost impossible for Sam to hold it any longer and he deep throated him before bobbing up and down over the whole length of Sam's cock, gripping it quite hard with his lips. The orgasm was the most intense Sam could ever remember. It was some time before he calmed down enough to do anything, and then he burst into tears.

"Oh Tom, that was absolutely amazing."

Phill was at his side in a second stroking his body to calm him down again. Tom watched the action and listened to the words of love that Phill whispered to his soul mate. All calm again and Tom spoke.

"You love each other very much, don't you?"

Sam, still snuffling a little replied.

"Yes, more than my life."

Phill thought about the blowjob and decided to be wicked.

"I think you are trying to seduce my lover with your incredible lovemaking ability, so I am going to punish you to show you that is not a good idea."

Sam and Tom looked at him, a little surprised until they saw the wicked look on Phill's face, barely covering a grin.

"I want you lying over your desk with your legs spread wide."

Tom did as he was told and Phill whispered to Sam.

"Get the lube from the bedroom. I'm going to open him up and spank him before sliding in to fuck him."

Phill took so much pleasure from slowly opening up Tom's anus, intermittently spanking him as well. He kept the slaps very soft so that they set up a tingle but didn't have enough power to bruise or cause any real pain. After about thirty, he used the lube on his own penis and Tom's ass before sliding in gently, all the way in one go as he felt Tom relax. He had never fucked anyone but Sam and Robbie, so this was an interesting experience. Tom was very good, working his gluts to make it better for Phill who had a mighty orgasm, but realised that doing it to Sam was much better because of the love.

"Now let that be a lesson to you." He said as he fell across Tom's back, sniggering. He felt round the front then and realised Tom had cum as well. Phill slid out of Tom and laughing said to him, "So you enjoyed that, did you?"

Tom stood up, turned round and planted a very passionate kiss on Phill's lips.

"Mmm, that was pretty damn good. I think you hit my prostate every time you went in and coupled with the tingle on the outside, it was sensational. Aren't you a clever boy? Who taught you that little move?"

Phill preened then.

"I've never done it before, it was just you talking about CP gave me the idea. Maybe I should try it on Sam next time."

Sam grinned, "Oh, yes please."

"I can see you are ready to go again, Sam, would you like to fuck our slave while he is still primed?"

Evil grin, but this time, Tom found himself on his bed with Sam between his legs and Phill holding them high and wide. He admitted afterwards that Sam had given him the best fuck he ever had.

"It was the thickness Sam. It didn't miss a millimetre of my insides as it slid in and out. Every nerve in my body reacted to it. You are a sensational top."

"Well, you have been a pretty sensational bottom, so now you can have us any way you like, Tom. I for one will be interested to feel your rod of iron and see how it compares to Sam's battering ram."

Consensus after Tom had made love to both the boys was that his experience showed, but Phill thought Sam was better and Sam thought Phill was better.

Tom looked at these two beautiful young men and was glowing with the pleasure he had taken from their bodies. Now he had to tell them.

"That is how it should be. You have no idea how sensational I think you both are and if you ever want to romp again with someone else, I will be delighted to oblige."

Phill, ever the extrovert looked at Sam.

"I think we might manage that occasionally, don't you Lover?"

Sam was pleased that Phill felt like that because he did as well. Monogamy was all very well, but sex with someone else as long as they were together did seem to be a fun way to expand their experience.

"Oh yes Phill, I never did it with anyone before you, but if you are with me I think it could be fun with others, and Tom is pretty special, isn't he?"

That opened the door to some marvellous orgies during the remainder of their college time. Usually organised by Tom, but very often involving as many as three other students. Phill and Sam loved it and Sam got a reputation as something special with his very thick monster cock.

Chapter 7

Harry watched with pride as his two sons graduated with firsts. At the reception afterwards, he listened to Tom Ryan laud their accomplishments on the field, and more important academically.

"You have every right to be immensely proud of your two sons, Colonel. They are a credit to you, and for me, they have been a delight to mentor for the last two years."

"Thank you Tom, and I think we can drop the Colonel. Harry I am sure will do. I understand that congratulations are due to you as well. A full professor now at only 32."

Tom blushed as he replied.

"Thank you Harry, but it was the group of students that I mentored that went a good way to me achieving that. Every one of them has graduated with a first."

Phill and Sam knew why. None of them had been into the party scene, just the sex orgies, which had left them all plenty of time to study.

Harry was now the commandant of an air base just outside Sacramento. The appointment would probably be good for four years, and then he hoped for his first star and an appointment to the Pentagon.

The boys now had to make a decision about what they were going to do. Sam wanted to study Constitutional law and go to the BAR. Phill wanted to do a doctorate in History. Now they had to find a college that would allow both of them to study their chosen subject.

Job done when they were accepted to a college on the East Coast, close to Washington. Was their good luck never going to end?

They would be in a position to start job hunting while they were still seeking their qualifications, because they would settle in or near Washington in anticipation of Harry being appointed there and Phill wanted to be close to his dad. Sam didn't care. He would live on the moon as long as he had Phill with him.

Plan A worked. Sam was meeting all of the right people who came to the college as visiting lecturers from legal firms in the Washington area. He researched each one to make sure that he applied to the most prestigious ones first.

All going to plan and with another honours degree to his credit, Sam went into action. Harry had his star and an appointment to the Pentagon, so Sam used that knowledge to bolster his CV. At interviews, he impressed, and was quite sure he was going to be offered a place with his first choice partnership. He was called for a second interview and sat with just one of the partners. Sam guessed he was the junior one because he was quite young.

"I have a generous offer on the table here, Sam. Whether I offer it to you on behalf of the senior partner is entirely my decision. We are prepared to take you on as an associate paralegal until you are accepted to the BAR. The path to a partnership is entirely in your hands, but if you perform well, you could have that before you are thirty. The starting salary is $36,000 plus benefits. When you pass the bar exam, that will double and you will be entitled to bonuses. A junior partnership will be worth not less than $100,000 plus bonuses, and if you match me, before you are thirty you will be grossing a million dollars a year."

Sam sat back gasping, those figures were almost too huge for him to grasp. It was only a few years ago that he was a penniless refugee from a war ravaged country. Now he lived in the house of an Air Force General, had a boyfriend he would die for and was being offered money beyond the desires of Croesus.

"Thank you, Sir. For that package I doubt there is anything I wouldn't do to make you offer it to me."

"You can drop the Sir, Sam. I'm Richard and will be your mentor while you study for the BAR. Getting my acceptance is going to be relatively easy, I hope. I would like you to strip for me and then stand in front of my desk with your feet positioned under your shoulders and your hands grasped behind your head."

Sam thought back to the early times with Tom and smiled. Richard picked up on it.

"Ok, so what's amusing?"

"I know I am up to the job without this, but the same thing applied when I wanted to be accepted at an American College. That mentor is now my dearest friend and despite my love for my partner, both of us will always consider it a pleasure if he wants to bed me again. I hope you are going to be the same, Richard."

"So you're gay, and who is your partner?"

"Phill Affleck, he's my brother by adoption. His father, sorry, our father has just been appointed to the Pentagon. General Harry Affleck."

Richard grinned, and then gulped. "You aren't going to have me thrown into a military prison if I plant my little Richard in your arse as a joining present, are you?"

Also grinning, Sam replied.

"Well, it will depend on how good you are."

Richard got serious then.

"You and your partner, Sam, are you normally monogamous?"

"Normally, yes, but we love a romp with friends if they are special. You needn't ask. I'm hoping you are going to be a special friend."

Richard grinned unreservedly.

"I'm going to try, so you can follow my order and I'm going to strip as well."

Sam was sure he had his first choice job now and a mentor with whom he would be perfectly in tune.

Naked, Richard was stunning. He had a well-defined body indicating he was no stranger to a gym. The back view had Sam very hard—he had a very cute butt. The cock would be no problem: it was average length and thickness, cut, with a small ball sac underneath.

'*I'll enjoy loosening that up,*' was Sam's thought. The face and hair were appropriate for a high flying lawyer and the whole picture was, in Sam's eyes, very sexy.

Richard walked round Sam when they were both naked, and gently stroked his torso before moving lower and playing with Sam's cock and balls. The erect appendage pleased him immensely.

"I hope you swing, Sam. I am going to plant my little Richard in your arse, but I hope yours will end up in mine occasionally as well. That is a stupendous piece of man-meat."

Richard sat back in his chair then and told Sam to demonstrate his ability to give blowjobs.

It would have been so easy to fail here if he hadn't liked Richard, but the reverse was the case and Sam showed him how good a blowjob could be, happily swallowing the discharge and sucking gently until the cock was completely soft.

"That was fantastic Sam. I know it is going to take me a while to recover, so why don't you lay me across my desk and fuck my brains out?"

As he spoke, Richard was removing a tube of gel from his desk drawer.

Sam didn't need to be asked twice and had to really concentrate not to cum until he had given Richard a really good seeing to.

"Oh fuck, Sam. You could be useless and I'd still sign you on. You suck like no one I have ever been with, and if that is how you fuck for a quickie, I think I'm going to kidnap you and have you by my bed for sex every day, several times a day."

Sam grinned. "Does that mean I have a job?"

Both men couldn't stop grinning as they cleaned up and dressed.

"You start the first of the month. I'll show you to your desk and give you all the blurb you need to read before your first day. I'd like to see you socially before then to meet your partner and your father, if possible. We like to think that we are a family-oriented firm and look after our staff accordingly because we know you will work long hours on occasion."

"I know Phill finishes college about four and gets back home about half five. Why don't we arrange to meet for a drink together one evening at a bar down town? That will break the ice and then I can invite you to dinner with the general one evening."

"I like that, Sam. Why not tomorrow evening? I know a very comfortable executive bar downtown we could meet early evening."

Arrangements complete and Sam wondered how Phill would react when he told him about the sex interview.

Of course it was no problem. Phill was as sure of Sam's love as Sam was of his, so it was curiosity that prompted Phill's questions.

"So, a cute butt. Maybe I'll get the chance to feel my little Phill caressing his insides as well."

"Huh, he'll never want mine again once he has felt your snake roaming round his lower regions. I won't mind, he can suck me while you are fucking his brains out."

Too much, and two young men were almost late for dinner with dad.

Harry was naturally delighted that Sam had his new position.

"I was sure that Phill made a good choice of life partner so I'm not surprised that I am so proud of you again."

Sam blushed.

"Thanks, Dad, I never want to let you down. The two of you have given me so much, I'll never stop loving you both."

Happy families again and Sam went to sleep in the arms of his man, contented like never before.

Sam was only a little apprehensive when they met Richard in the bar the following evening. He needn't have been. They hit it off immediately and spent a pleasant couple of hours discovering each other's life stories. Phill was going to do historical research as an assistant professor once he had his doctorate, which should happen in a few months when his thesis was complete. Dinner with Harry a few nights later cemented the relationship as friends.

Sam started work, immediately feeling the advantage of a good personal relationship with Richard. A summons to Richard's office just before lunch one day set the tone for the future.

"I want you naked and comfortable in the armchair, Sam."

Richard remained clothed, but slid between Sam's legs and gave him a superb blowjob, making him gasp.

"To be honest with you Sam. I'm more of a bottom than a top, so the chances are you'll get loads of blowjobs and when we can make it, you'll be lodging your baby maker in my butt. I guess we'll 69 when we get the chance so you'll be taking nutrition from me occasionally as well."

Sam loved this. He was glowing when he joined the partners for lunch, and the knowing looks that passed between them made him realise that they were all in the know on this one. He blushed initially but was soon put at his ease. He did wonder if this kind of thing was general practice, having experienced it in college. He was sure all of the partners were not gay, but as most men were not completely gay or straight, he could imagine a mainly straight man taking delight in reaming out another guy's arse. He wondered if he would be expected to attend to any of the other partners or if he was going to be the exclusive property of Richard. One way to find out: Ask.

After lunch, Sam returned to Richard's office with him and put the question.

"We have 63 partners, Sam. You will almost certainly be 64th. I would guess that about half of them are gay. I think the reason it is such a high percentage is that unlike the jocks at college, we tended to spend more time in sex than parties and left ourselves more time to study. The boss is 100% straight, but he realised the potential of gay guys: we don't need time off for kids events; if we have partners, they are generally less pain when we work long hours than wives and girlfriends are; and finally, because we handle a load of discrimination cases, usually high profile ones, he wanted partners that were genuinely sympathetic to the cause."

Nodding his understanding, Sam responded.

"So I suppose I am going to have to keep Phill sweet when I tell him of my sexual exploits, not just with you, but with some of the other partners as well?"

"Not necessarily. They will respect it if you say no, but you will get much more help if you go with the flow."

"I'm going with the flow, whatever that entails, because I want to pass the BAR the first time, and by my work rate and achievement, make partner as soon as it is possible to do."

"You'll do it as well, I'm sure. You majored in Constitutional Law and that is an area we are weak on in this firm."

Chapter 8

The first exposure to the partners for Phill came at a late summer BBQ for the partners and their significant others. Sam and Phill received invitations as well, which Sam realised was exceptional. This was an endorsement of his position in the firm after only three months. Several of the partners had same sex attachments but it was very relaxed, and Phill, as a new PhD, was quite happy in this intellectual company. It was quite obvious early in the day that both Phill and Sam were the subject of lustful glances, from quite a few sources and invitations to join conversations.

"I think my sex life is about to take another leap forward, my love. I hope you aren't going to get upset."

Phill sniggered.

"Are you kidding? I get so turned on when you tell me what you and Richard have done, on the floor, over the desk, in the armchairs. It all gives us so much ammunition for experimentation. I ought to volunteer to join you."

Sam laughed.

"We could easily become true fuck and suck sluts couldn't we?"

Phill became serious with his reply.

"Variety is the spice of life. As long as you love only me, I'm quite content with whatever turns up."

Love affirmed and they re-joined other conversations.

Addison Graham was another of the constitutional law experts and was very friendly towards both Phill and Sam.

"I think you are going to be my paralegal, Sam, in a case coming up soon. It's quite a high profile discrimination case that overlaps with the constitution. I think you and I can make the defence squirm on this one. Come and see me Monday."

Turning off business very quickly, Addison turned to Phill and asked about his job. He was very friendly and complimentary about his work, leaving both guys with a positive image of this very handsome black partner. The little goatee beard added to the distinguished look that was carried on a slim body.

Successful exposure at this partners get together, and on the Monday, a successful start to Sam's association with Addison professionally. He realised that the knowledge he would gain from this case would be priceless when he sat the BAR exam.

During a break from work mid-morning, Addison asked Sam about Phill.

"How long have you and Phill been together?"

Sam replied, "I met him at school in England just after the war. I was a refugee from the Philippines. His father adopted me and we have been together ever since. College in California to start with, and then here in Washington so that we could be close to Phill's dad when, as we expected, he got his star and an appointment to the Pentagon."

"You are both very lucky then, because if I didn't know better, I wouldn't put either of you older than 21."

"Thanks Addison, I know Phill would be flattered. I never think of it, but we both stay in shape so I haven't noticed any change in him, really, except for a little more maturity."

"I liked him very much when we met at the weekend. I'd like you both to come to dinner at my apartment sometime."

Sam was still a little naïve because he didn't read any ulterior motive into that request.

Addison Graham was mid-thirties, one of only a handful of black partners, gay and promiscuous. More interested in variety than a meaningful relationship. He was married to the law and had a reputation as a very hard worker, clocking loads of chargeable hours on every case he worked on.

"I'm a workaholic, Sam, but I don't expect you to clock up the same hours as I do. You have a life with Phill; this job is my life. I sleep here nearly as often as I sleep at home."

Sam was intrigued, and quizzed Richard about it when he got the chance. Apparently, there were three suites on the top floor where the senior partner's offices were, and they were used by partners that worked long hours on particular cases.

The first indication Sam had that Addison was interested in some carnal knowledge of him was one lunch time.

"I have asked the catering staff to put two lunches in Suite A upstairs. Let's eat in comfort today, Sam."

The lunches were just finger snacks. Heavy lunches slowed one down in the afternoons; and that wasn't a good idea from the partnership's point of view. Finished and relaxing, Addison spoke.

"Richard tells me you have a quite astounding body and groin, Sam. Would you strip for me so that I can view it for myself?"

Sam was not comfortable with this. It was okay with Richard for some reason, probably because they were close in age and had bonded so quickly. Addison was a nice guy and had been a huge help to Sam even though he pulled his weight as well. He knew he could refuse, but he was still thinking BAR exam, and this guy's knowledge would be invaluable. So he did. He stood up in front of Addison and peeled his clothes off. Stood naked and flaccid, Addison stood up, moved in close and gently teased Sam to a good solid erection.

"Richard was correct. You are one very sexy young man, and that cock is to die for. Fair is fair. Why don't you undress me now?"

Sam grinned. Now this he could handle. He had never been close up to a naked black man, and he guessed he was going to see him erect as well. Job done and Sam was mouth agape looking at Addison's groin. His cock was about nine inches long and only chubbed up.

"Come through to the bedroom and you can play."

Addison squatted on the bed. Sam was able to comfortably kneel in front of him and start playing. When Addison was erect, Sam could hardly believe it. The cock was easily twelve inches long, circumcised and not heavily veined, nor was it too thick, not as thick as his in fact.

"That is a cock to be proud of Addison. I have never seen anything even come close to it in length. I always gauge cock size against Phill who is pretty impressive, but yours is stupendous." Addison smiled, laid back on the bed to one side.

"In that case, why don't you give it the taste test and I will do the same to you."

Sam didn't have any misgivings. Sucking this guy was an amazing experience and he loved that Addison was sucking him as well. When fingers wandered to his anal entry and penetrated him, Sam was so turned on that he didn't object. He was beginning to space out at all the stimulation, so he was putty in Addison's hands when a few minutes later he was rolled onto his tummy and Addison told him to come up on his knees, keep his shoulders on the bed, and spread his legs wide. Sam nearly hit the roof when Addison's tongue started working his anus, interposed with fingers. His senses appeared to be heightened so he immediately felt the change when Addison placed his glans at the entrance to Sam's butt.

"Relax now Baby, and this won't hurt."

He was right, it didn't hurt. Addison was not a whole lot thicker than Phill. The penetration felt amazing and even when it went into his large intestine, he was fine because Phill did the same. When it felt different was the continued penetration until he thought he was going to be licking the head from the inside. He had never felt so full.

"You have me all now, Baby. Just relax, you're doing fine."

Addison was surprised that Sam had taken him so easily. *'Phill must be pretty long himself,'* was his thought. Perhaps he would get the chance to find out when they came to dinner. He slow-fucked Sam for ages before rolling him over, pushing his legs down by the thighs until they were resting on the bed either side of his shoulders, then he went for maximum penetration and a few hard strokes until he deposited a huge load deep inside Sam's ass. Sam squealed at the combination of pain and pleasure, but had his own very intense orgasm. Gasping for breath, he looked at the very satisfied expression on Addison's face.

"You are very wicked, taking advantage of this poor innocent paralegal."

Addison fell sideways alongside Sam, laughing like an idiot.

"Yes, I noted how much you disliked this. I suppose that is why you took twelve inches as though it was a daily occurrence. Just how long is Phill?"

"Mmm, close to ten inches I guess."

Cleaning up ready to go back to work, both men had a fit of the giggles.

Addison got serious going back down in the lift.

"This isn't going to be a problem for you with Phill, is it?"

Sam smiled. "Nope. If I describe that session in enough detail he, will probably fuck my brains out tonight at least twice."

Surprised reply, "You mean you are going to tell him everything?"

"Oh yes," Sam replied, "I have no secrets from Phill, not now, not ever."

"Wow, that is some relationship. I shall be awfully embarrassed now if I have you both to dinner."

"You needn't be, Richard and Phill are quite good friends now and I told him everything when Richard took advantage of me."

Addison shook his head. This was new territory for him in the human relationships front.

Sam knew he had been right not to make a fuss over the sex thing. It didn't happen again at work with Addison, and by the time the case was heard in court, which they won, he had garnered so much new knowledge on constitutional and human rights law that he could have studied for months and not gained the same amount of knowledge.

He sat his BAR exam a couple of months later and sailed through it. The partners had done the same thing with other sections of the law as they had done with Addison. The party they had for him after the results were known brought tears of pleasure to Sam's eyes. It was only the partners and senior associates who attended in the company conference room, with outside caterers putting on a stupendous finger buffet. Champagne was the only drink served and Sam had to make a speech. He had made a few in mock trials in law school, but this was much more difficult. He thanked the senior partner for giving him the opportunity to join such a prestigious law practice, and he thanked individually the partners he had worked with who had imparted so many words of wisdom.

"I know that a good speech should have an amusing beginning and an amusing end, with the two being as close together as possible, so I am sorry if I rambled on a little, but you all have been so incredibly helpful, I had to tell you. Thank you, thank you, and thank you."

The tears of happiness and gratitude came then, and the triumvirate of senior partners looked at each other and nodded their approval of this young refugee that had endeared himself to an Air Force General sufficiently to be adopted by him, and to all his colleagues here who had given off their time freely to help this personable young man.

Sam was gushing as he told Phill and Harry about it that night.

"I'm sure you deserved it Son. I think they are very lucky to have you in their organisation."

"Here, here," said Phill as he patted Sam on the back.

In bed that night, Phill showed his soul mate how proud of him he was, reducing him to tears of joy again.

Epilogue

Two years later, Phill was awarded a full professorship, Harry picked up his second star and Sam became the youngest partner in the firm's history.

When Harry retired from the Air Force, Phill and Sam bought a house in the suburbs of Washington that had a self-contained apartment in one wing. They pleaded with Harry to move in and keep them company, which he did with pleasure, taking over the running of the house and gardens.

Phill was appointed Dean of his college on his fiftieth birthday, and Sam, a few months later, became senior partner in the firm that he had joined as a law graduate.

The practice of indoctrinating new boys into gay sex continued under Sam's leadership—always emphasising the voluntary aspect. No straight boy suffered by saying no, and no gay boy ever felt pressured by it.

Sam and Phill had become monogamous soon after Sam's partnership had been taken up.

"I don't need to screw around with young graduates Phill. That was fun when we were younger, but loving sex is all I need now."

Phill had never indulged other than with Sam and now was content with their lives. He had experienced one minor orgy with Addison who had felt obliged to let both young men fuck him after he had taken his pleasure with Phill.

Robbie McCormack and Tom Ryan remained lifelong friends and all met up at different times and places throughout the years.

Both of them always expressed a desire to go to bed with Sam and Phill on each visit. It never happened, but did make for loads of hilarity.

Sam became a very high profile supporter and crusader for equal rights for same sex partners, ably supported by Phill who included lectures on the subject in his history classes.

The only cloud in their lives after declaring their love for each other as teenagers, was the death of Harry. The boys were retired by then as well, so the distress at his parting was tempered with the thought that he had lived to a fine old age in great health and had simply died when his body was worn out.

The End

WANT FREE COPIES OF MY BOOKS?

Just visit my blog and download free copies of my books:
http://dexter-chase.awesomeauthors.org/dexter-chase/

Here is a sample from another story you may enjoy:

Gay Romance

Dexter Chase

Love on the High Seas

"Wakey, wakey, Chief, it's 0345."

I groaned—but sat up in my bunk, turning on the bunk light as I did so. It was shielded so that it wouldn't disturb anyone else. Sleep shorts off, briefs on and then my overalls. Socks and shoes and then it was off to the heads (naval terminology for the bathroom) to wash and clean my teeth. I carried with me my bucket—yes, chief of the watch in the engine room of one of Her Majesty's destroyers, and I carried a bucket on watch with me. In the bucket was my washing gear, my dirty overalls, socks from my last watch and some washing powder.

The morning watch started at 0400 and as I slid down the ladder to the control platform, I was greeted by the chief I was relieving, holding a steaming mug of hot chocolate.

"We're steaming on both boilers, Baz. The second one came on line about half an hour ago. Officer of the watch says we are starting early morning manoeuvres at 0500. Presently set at 132 revs. I've signed off the log. See you later."

He was up the ladder and I bet less than ten minutes later, he would be asleep in his bunk.

I took my first sip of the hot chocolate and sighed. I hated the morning watch but I loved the hot chocolate. I checked the log and turned to my two stoker mechanics.

"Mac, bearing check straight away. Danny, take these down to the bottom plates and put them to wash."

My bucket would be half filled with water, washing powder distributed, and then a steam drain, from one of the auxiliary turbine pumps buried in it and cracked, to boil them.

I was a first class engine room artificer and an anomaly in my branch. Instead of looking like I had just crawled out of the bilges (which most of my colleagues did), I was always clean and smart when I went to work. I wore overalls almost all the time at sea and mine were always super clean at the start of my watch or my day duty. Even my shoes had shine to them; again, almost the only pair in my branch that did. My boss was always telling me I was too smart to be a 'tiffi'; I should bugger off to the wardroom, that is, become an officer. I thought about it, but I was only 22, the youngest engine room artificer, first class, in the navy. That gave me the rank of Chief Petty Officer. Nobody liked me outside of my branch because of the age thing.

My two watch mechanics were Mac and Danny. They had been with me for about six months ever since we left England for the Far East. Danny was the youngest at eighteen and took his cue from me. He was always smart as well. Mac was older by a few years and was as reliable as I could wish for. If a bearing was running a little warm, he would tell me; he religiously checked oil levels on his rounds; and when he was on the plates of the control platform with me, he scanned the instruments just like me, always pointing out if a gauge reading had moved from where he thought it should be. I liked both of these guys and I like to think it was reciprocated.

I carried a dark secret, though—with regard to Danny. I fancied him something wicked. He was absolutely gorgeous. I had never said anything to him about my feelings, and had always tried to treat him the same as any other mechanic, but it was difficult. When we were on day duties, I nearly always had him with me and taught him a lot more than I needed to, trying to help him with his exams for leading hand.

The year was 1963—and being gay was a crime in civil life and so taboo in the navy that if anyone was caught in a homosexual liaison, it was a court marshal and seven years in a civil jail.

We entered Singapore and tied up alongside a depot ship. The maintenance teams on there would help us with our mini refit. Now, I had a chance to progress my liaison with Danny, if he was of like mind. I casually invited Danny and Mac to go ashore with me the night after we docked, already knowing that Mac had pulled the duty watch.

Danny came with me and we headed for Bughi Street in Singapore City. Lots of bars, naughty ladies and transvestites. It was fun and we drank more than perhaps we should have done. Both of us could stay ashore until we had to report for duty the next morning, so I thought rather than risk getting in trouble for being drunk (not that we were), we stayed at the Britannia Club. The little rooms were okay and Danny's was next to mine. I led him into his; and because he was a little tipsy, I thought, I should help him undress. When he was down to his boxers, he just stood there and looked at me. I moved in close to him, and looking him in the eyes, I slowly lowered his boxers. He didn't resist, so I dropped to my knees and helped him get rid of them from around his ankles. His cock was just about level with my head, so I leant in and just kissed the end of it before standing up. We held eye contact and I moved my head close to his and kissed him on the lips.

That was it. He threw his arms round my neck and gave me a kiss that nearly made me collapse.

"I've wanted to do that for so long it was driving me crazy."

I realised when he said that that he wasn't slurring his words anymore.

"You're not tipsy?"

He laughed. "Nowhere near. But this was the only way that I could think of for you to get my clothes off. Can I undress you now?"

If you enjoyed this sample then look for <u>Love On The High Seas</u>.

Also by this Author:

Mastered

Go For Goal Or... Guy?

Ruin

The Loser

Forced by the Military

Lucifer's Academy

So Full It Hurts!

Bully to Slave

Play & Pretend

The Submissive Bad Boy

Unexpected Island Mates

No Hoper

Chance of the Heart

Boy Beauty Contest

Finding Michael

Caribbean Fun

Bareback On Board

Weird Arrangement

Love on the High Seas

About the Author

Dexter Chase is a writer of hot, gay erotica stories in both paperback and Kindle versions.

His very first book published is <u>Mastered (Sensual Tales from Ancient Egypt)</u> which is about an eighteen-year old Ajax, who was taken as a slave and brought to a great house by a high-ranking soldier.

Check out his books and you'll enjoy extreme gay erotica of all time.

You may also like the books by these authors:

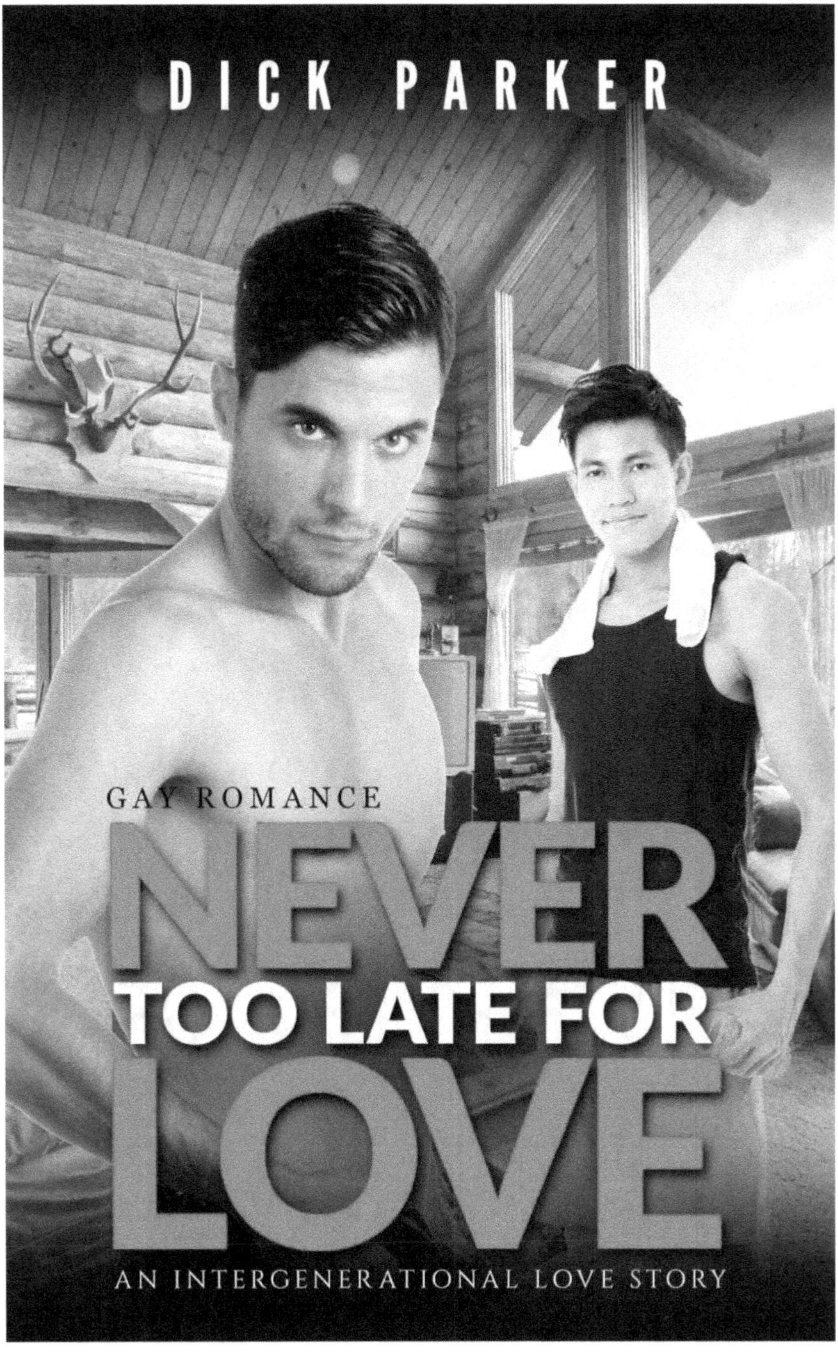
DICK PARKER
GAY ROMANCE
NEVER
TOO LATE FOR
LOVE
AN INTERGENERATIONAL LOVE STORY

"Do you have an appointment?"

"I've never been in a massage place before," I said. "I didn't know I needed one."

"Most of the time we need appointments. But we had a cancellation and I could fit you in. That is, if you don't mind being massaged by another man."

I hadn't expected that but actually it kind of made me feel more comfortable. "That's fine," I said.

She went back behind a curtain and a minute later she came back followed by a boy. He was beautiful. He looked like he was part Asian and maybe part Hispanic. He was small but very well built with smooth dark skin, shiny black hair and brown eyes. His face was angelic. He smiled at me and his smile was beautiful.

"This is Tran."

I nodded to the kid. "I'm Charlie. Charlie Dodge," I said.

"The fee is $50 for one half hour. If you are satisfied you may tip your masseur," the woman said.

I handed her $50.

"Please follow me, Mr. Dodge," the kid said.

He was wearing black silk shorts and a white strap undershirt and flip-flops. I guessed him at about five-foot five and maybe a hundred twenty pounds. His hair was longish and cut in a boyish style that hung over his ears and down his back a bit. He had bangs in front.

I followed him and took a good look at his cute ass. Damn the kid had a hell of an ass on him. He was cute as hell but way too young.

We went in a little room with a waist- high narrow bed that was covered with a thin mat and a sheet. There was a table with oils and things on it and a stack of towels.

"Would you like me to step out while you undress?" he asked.

"I have to get completely naked?"

"Only if you choose. What part of your body do you wish to have worked on?"

I explained about my side and shoulder.

"You may keep your pants on if you wish. You would probably be more comfortable without them, but it is your choice."

I thought about it for a second. What the hell? How often did I get a chance to get naked in front of a hot little shit like this?

I took off my shirt, and shoes and socks. Then I dropped my jeans and boxers and stepped out of them. He looked. But then he patted the bed and I lay on it flat on my stomach. He put a little towel over my ass. He traced his fingers over my scar. It ran from my shoulder blade down about nine inches to my side.

"What happened?" he asked.

I explained the surgery.

"They opened your lung?"

"I was a sick man."

"Is it very painful? I am afraid to touch it."

"The scar is fine. It's down under where it hurts. They cut some ribs and then put in a thing they called a spreader. It's like a device that they crank open so they can get their hands in there to work on me. The spreader crushed all the nerves and muscles and tendons. That's why I'm so sore."

"I will be very careful."

He put some warm oil on my back and I felt his soft hands touching me. He lightly worked on the area and it felt really nice. "Am I hurting you?"

"No it feels nice. You can do it a bit harder if you want."

He worked the place harder. It gave me a twinge of pain now and then, but it really felt nice most of the time. "You have wonderful hands, Tran."

"Thank you, Mr. Dodge."

"Call me Charlie."

"Yes, Mr. Charlie."

I laughed.

He worked me for quite a while. Then I started getting a little sore from the muscles being rubbed.

"I think that's enough for today," I said.

"You still have ten minutes left of time."

"Well, that's okay," I said.

"I could do your shoulders and back. You feel tense."

"Sure," I said.

He put oil on my shoulders and back and began massaging them. Oh man, the kid knew what he was doing. He squeezed and rubbed and it felt amazing. Then he moved down and did my legs. He was working on the back of my thighs next. Damn, his hands were like warm butter. His hands were up on the top of my thighs and then where they moved to turned into butt.

"Would you like me to go a bit higher?"

Oh man.

"If I have time left, sure."

He took the towel off my ass. He put a little oil on my ass cheeks and kneaded them like two balls of bread dough. Damn, it felt good… and I started getting a hard-on.

"I think that's enough, Tran," I said.

"Let me wipe the oil off," he said.

He took a towel and wiped me down. Then he said I could get up. I had a semi-boner so I tried to keep my back to him. He put the towel in a hamper and when he turned back he looked at my half-hard cock.

If you enjoyed this sample then look for <u>Never Too Late For Love</u>.

NAUGHTY GAY EROTICA

PLAY
& Pretend

DEXTER CHASE

Jack had been watching Evan for weeks at the start of the new soccer season. Mostly, the observation was carried out in the locker and shower rooms after football practice. Evan was the new boy, started at the beginning of year eleven, but a year older than most. Jack had befriended him from the start, but not purely for altruistic reasons. To Jack's eyes, Evan was simply gorgeous. The girls had started to swarm round him like bees round a honey pot, but he never hitched up with one of them. Jack thought that was very strange, and started his observation campaign. He noted that Evan was nearly always first in the shower, and chose the shower head in the corner that allowed him to keep his genitals hidden, if he wanted to, but able to scope out everyone else in the showers. He was nearly always last out and, once again, Jack noted why. Evan sported a very chubby cock, not quite erect, so he obviously had learnt to control it.

When Jack was convinced that Evan's actions weren't accidental, he followed suit, and arrived in the showers in time to see Evan's cock completely flaccid. It was still an impressive size, confirming in Jack's mind that it would grow into a monster. He waited on one occasion until the locker room was nearly empty before approaching Evan.

"Quite a few impressive pieces of equipment, don't you think, Evan?"

Evan blushed, and couldn't look directly at Jack.

"What do you mean?"

"Come on Ev, I've seen you scope out the guys. You must know, to the millimeter, the length of every flaccid cock in the first and second elevens."

Evan vehemently denied it.

"That denial doesn't wash buddy; I've watched you for too long. You must know, by now, that yours is the longest, by quite a lot. If you are a grower and not a shower, it is probably a ten-incher, which is pretty impressive."

Evan was pleased with that comment, and impressed with Jack's accuracy. He was almost exactly ten inches, and he was very proud of it.

They finished dressing and left the locker room to head home. Jack knew that they only lived one road apart, so to Evan's surprise, Jack stuck with him.

"Do you live this way, Jack?"

"Yeah, Moscow Road."

"I only live one road beyond... in Crimea Crescent."

"Really? Would you like to drop off at my house for a while? We could do our assignments together and then have a talk."

Evan smelled a rat.

"What do you want to talk about?"

"Oh, nothing much; school, soccer, how you're fitting in as the new boy."

Evan shrugged, "Ok."

The first bit went fine; doing assignments together worked well, because two brains were better than one.

Jack got up from his chair and stretched, before removing his shirt and tie. Then he toed off his shoes and bent to take off his socks. When he stood up, he undid his belt, undid the button at the waist, and pulled down the zip, slipping the trousers over his hips, dropping them to the floor and, again, bending to pick them up, but this time with his back to Evan. Through his legs, he saw Evan's eyes looking at his butt. After he had hung the trousers, he sat back down, making sure that by slipping down on the chair it forced his boxers up tight in his crotch, clearly outlining his cock down his left leg. Again, Evan's eyes looked at the display before looking up at Jack and blushing, realising he had been caught.

"See something you like, Ev?"

Evan gulped and then tried to brazen it out.

"Not really; just wondering why you have stripped off."

"I like to be comfortable when I'm chilling out in my room. Besides, mum and dad won't be in for another couple of hours, so I get to beat off in comfort without worrying about being disturbed."

While he was talking, Jack had been stroking his cock through his boxers, and it had grown considerably, and continued to grow when he put his hands behind his head. Evan gulped, and looked very uncomfortable as he kept taking quick glances at the growing appendage. He tried to adjust his own growing cock without Jack noticing, and failed completely.

"Now I think you see something that you like, and it's got you all excited."

If you enjoyed this sample then look for **Play & Pretend**.

Here Comes Trouble

Becoming Gay Erotica

ANGUS MacGregor

Sitting on this ridge top, I wonder why in the hell I ever agreed to come on this elk hunt. I don't really even like hunting. I used to, but not so much anymore. I mean, I love the camaraderie, and being outside in Oregon, and the beer. I love the beer the most. The whiskey is pretty great as well. I love the way the mist and clouds hug the mountains of the coast range like an old lady wearing a fur. The carpet of endless green, an ocean of Douglas fir that slides down the hills and tucks in and around rock outcroppings and pulls up its skirts for the rivers to splash through. The smell of wood smoke and the crisp autumn air that is just waiting to turn blue and bathe the mountains in frigid winter. But something is up with this hunting trip. It has been strange since the minute we got on the road. What am I saying? It's been weird for months.

Now that I am paying attention, and if I am honest, it's been going on since Emma and I met back in college. I dreaded the whole – "meet the parents" thing. I'm a real outgoing guy, not shy in the least. I don't have any confidence issues either. I mean, I'm lucky enough to have good looks and the kind of personality that most people seem comfortable with. But it's different meeting the parents. There's a whole other level of scrutiny and judgment that be part of that.

But I should back up, because this story began months before that, shit, it was years. I was the baby of my family, Chad Alonzo Martinez. A big brown-eyed, black haired, tanned little ball of energy. I had a brother that was ten years older than me. I adored him, but he and I had zero in common and hardly spent any time together at all. I was barely in grade school when he was graduating from high school. I did get to spend about a year in his bedroom before he moved out. See, I had a sister too, and she and I had shared a bedroom for quite a while, but as she got older, she was done with having a younger brother in the middle of her business. Jack said he didn't mind, which looking back, I find hard to believe. He was practically a grown man and I was just this cute little boy. But back then, I went to bed so early, he was rarely in the room with me. He came to bed way after me and I was always up and out of the room before he starts stirring since he didn't have a first period class.

There were a few nights I woke up in the middle of the night to look over and see him stroking his cock fast and furious. I knew better than to interrupt something so obviously private. But I would lay still and watch in fascination as his hand moved silently up and down his huge penis. His eyes would close and he would fondle his balls, belly, and nipples as he jacked. A few times, I even saw him seemingly slide a finger up his ass, which was both mystifying and utterly shocking at the same time. In the end, he would raise his furry ass off the mattress and send a fat rope of semen blasting up on his hairy chest and belly. He would usually grab some scandalously grimy cum rag from underneath the bed and wipe off his chest and then turn over and begin to snore. I had no idea what the whole thing meant, but it was fascinating nonetheless. A few years later, I followed in his footsteps and began rubbing one off every night before sleeping, secretly thinking my older brother for the lesson he didn't even know he was providing.

There were a few conversations that also contributed to my sexual education. Jack tended to take really long showers, probably because he was masturbating the whole time in there as well. Very often, I would be brushing my teeth or taking a little boy dump when he would open up the curtain and step out of the shower in all his muscled, hairy glory. Most often, his penis would be still erect and I would watch astonished as it bobbed and bounced on top of impossibly huge testicles. Several times he caught me watching and made a point to walk over and rub my face in his crotch, playfully, but all the same, shocking for a little kid. Sometimes he would reach down and grab my penis or nuts and give them a playful squeeze and say, something ridiculous.

"Damn, little bro, your dick is almost as big as mine. You are gonna be hung like a horse by the time you are in high school."

If you enjoyed this sample then look for **Here Comes Trouble**.

A MAN'S TOY

HOT GAY EROTICA

AMY REDEK

I've still got the toy I was given when I was born and in growing up found that other boys had the same toy that I had, and in the process of getting older, still played with our toys.

I never knew my father because he was in the army and was killed somewhere in Northern India while serving his country. I was born a month after he had left and so it was only my mother that looked after me until I was able to look after myself. Which was quite early considering that mom, when I was old enough, around four years old, was to be looked after in a small crèche while she went to work in a munitions factory at the outbreak of what was known as "The Second World War".

I was taken there in the morning before she went to work and collected me in the early evening to take me home to feed, bathe and put me to bed, only having a Sunday to spend the whole day with me. I cannot say that I remember much of this, only one thing stands out clear was having to spend one night in a bomb shelter and was told later that I had cried so much that we never went into one again. We were lucky to be on the outskirt of London and so didn't have to suffer the bombing that the capital suffered.

It was a good thing that when I was five, I only had to be taken to school on that first day and from there on, went on my own and returned home well before mom came in from work.

As I grew older, I began to learn how to cook a meal so that she didn't have to worry about me being home alone and I think she appreciated having her dinner cooked for her. She had been heartbroken when she was informed that her husband had died in battle but still had me to remember him by and didn't marry again until I was sixteen.

I didn't like her choice and so stayed out of the house as much as possible, for I could never call him dad or father. I had left school at fifteen and found work as an errand boy and with this arrival of another man in the house, found a job for the evenings. This was in a hotel in the city and would start at mid-day until eight in the evening, travelling backwards and forwards by the underground train. I liked Saturdays, for they usually had functions there and so would do the extra hours until it finished and would then sleep in the cloakroom and work the Sunday morning until the afternoon, where I would then go to a cinema to watch whatever film was being shown before going home.

It was during this time that I learned that even though the country would be stopping conscription into the army sometime in the future, I would still be liable to being called up when I was eighteen. Now I could volunteer to join either the army or navy before the time arrived of my eighteenth birthday or enter the Merchant Navy, though that would mean being in there for seven years as opposed to only two in the army. The Royal Navy was seven years too, but more restrictive than the Merchant Navy, so that was what I planned to join.

I got the necessary papers finally and it took some time to get my mom to sign them, even though she knew that by me going to sea I would soon be leaving home, but also didn't want me to join the army and maybe having to go out and fight like my father had, so she signed them.
Now with the man she had married and herself, she always left home around seven thirty in the morning while I stayed in bed until they had gone before getting up. Seeing to my own breakfast, as not having to be at the hotel until mid-day, I would always see what the postman dropped through our letterbox. The day finally came when there was one brown envelope from the government that I knew would contain the order for me to do my National Service. This was three months before I would be eighteen, and so I wrote on the envelope that the person this letter was for, no longer lived at this address and posted it back on my way to take the signed paperwork to the office where they would see me to joining the Merchant Navy.

As I was still only seventeen, I would have to attend a navy school, which was at Gravesend, and they would let me know by letter the date to attend there. It was to take a course of six weeks and on passing, would be allocated to a ship. It was a month before this letter arrived giving me the date to attend this school, which was another four weeks later. This meant that I would then be eighteen by the time I finished at the school and would therefore not be classed as a boy rating. Oh, it was the catering department that I had applied for as opposed to being a deck hand for if I would be at sea in a winter time, it would be warmer being on the inside of the ship than out on deck.

In the meantime, another letter had come from the government asking mom where I might be contacted for my joining the army. She showed me this and didn't quite know what to say in reply. I told her to just say that I had since joined the Merchant Navy. So that cleared that problem.

I'd already given in my notice to the hotel that I would soon be leaving to join the navy and had a little party given me on my last day working there as I would on the following Monday have to report to the Gravesend school. Mom was in tears on that day when I left at six a.m., consoling her by saying that I would be back in six weeks' time before having to finally go to sea.

I duly turned up at the school on time, following others with their suitcases and saw that it looked like a prison that we would be spending the next six weeks in. In fact, it had once been a prison. One for women. There were twenty of us that lined up once we were inside and with me being at least a foot taller than the others, was made the senior of half of the group with another tall boy being the senior of the other half. We were to keep control of the others during our stay there. What a dump. Ten of us in a small dismal, filthy room that had five double bunks for us to sleep in. It only had one window that was filthy so the light had to be on even when it was daylight outside.

It definitely seemed like a prison, being woken up in the morning by the officer in charge of us, making a racket in the room and shouting out, "Hands off cocks and hands on socks" every morning at five thirty. This would give us thirty minutes to fight at the washbasins, three of them, to wash and clean our teeth before breakfast at six. Seven o'clock we would be in a class to then be shown what was expected of us.

How to make a bed navy fashion, which wasn't far off how I had been making mine for quite a few years. How to lay a table for meals, the same here too and so on. The names of a ship's interior: the floor being the deck, the ceiling a deckhead, the walls being bulkheads and many other names used aboard. The pecking order of the officers and of the stripes on their shoulders and what we had to wear when doing a daily chore and the change when we were seeing to passengers.

It was bad at first but we all got used to it and we all did well with our final tests at what we had been taught, and I got a good report from the officer that had been teaching us, rating me as excellent and top of our class. On our last day at the school, I was told that because I would then be eighteen by the time it came for me to report to a ship, I would be rated as being a steward, and would inside a week or too, know what ship I was to join and where.

I think we were all relieved to be leaving this prison to return to our homes to await our letters. Mom was pleased to see me though I wasn't sure about the man who had married her. I think he was glad that I would soon be leaving for good, little did he know that there would be times when I had ship's leave to spend there.

Though he did give me a present on my birthday, me thinking at first that he was taking the piss when I saw that it was a bible. But then he showed me how to open the inside cover that would be the ideal place to keep any money I had for if things were to be stolen on board ship, a bible would be the last thing that would be taken, and he was right. For things did tend to suddenly disappear from our cabins when in port and yet my bible was left alone. So overall, it wasn't a bad little party we had to celebrate me now being regarded as a man.

It wouldn't be long before I would learn how other men who not only played with their toys, but also what they did with them.

If you enjoyed this sample then look for **A Man's Toy**.

Keith Yates

Coach's
Private Lessons

Hot Gay Erotica

"YES, you are," Coach said in a commanding tone. "Your fucking hand had better be around my cock in the next few seconds or all deals are off. I will take these images to the Dean and have him deal with this situation. I am sure he will have to call your parents in and show them what their boy has been doing at school. Hell, it may have to even go before the board."

TJ could feel his heart sinking at the thought of his parents seeing him jacking off. Not to mention the Dean and the board. Fuck, he was so screwed.

"Soon everyone will know what you have been doing. How easy do you think it will be for you to land a new girlfriend then? Not to mention what your teammates will think of you."

He knew it was all true. He would be the laughing stock of the school. No girls would date him. The team would tease and torment him forever. He had little choice. He would have to - have to stroke Coach. TJ's own cock jumped at the thought of touching Coach's man post.

"Now get to work on my cock!" The command in the Coach's voice left little room for argument.

Looking up at the man TJ sighed. "Is there no other way?"

"NO!" Coach said. His tone left no doubt that TJ had one option.

TJ reached up and began rubbing the thick meat through the fabric of his shorts. He could feel the heat of the swollen man meat. Feel the wetness of the pre cum on the fabric of the shorts.

"Fucking do it right," Coach ordered. "Take my fucking cock out and wrap your fingers around it and fucking stroke me properly."

TJ slowly lowered Coach's shorts and jockey briefs revealing his large man cock. It was thick and long had to be close to 2 or 3 inches longer than TJ's own cock. Not to mention thick and pre cum was leaking from the big mushroom head.

Coach let the shorts slide down his legs and to the floor. His cock throbbed as TJ finally reached out and took it in his hand. He could feel the boy's hand shake a bit as he grasp the rock hard slab of meat...

If you enjoyed this sample then look for **Coach's Private Lessons**.

WANT FREE COPIES OF MY BOOKS?

Just visit my blog and download free copies of my books:
http://dexter-chase.awesomeauthors.org/dexter-chase/

www.ingramcontent.com/pod-product-compliance
Lightning Source LLC
Chambersburg PA
CBHW071408170626
46811CB00003B/1317